Audrey Carnegie, who was born in Jamaica has travelled the globe but lives her life in the UK, where she arrived at the age of seven. She has been described as mother of many but only gave birth to two.

Audrey is adventurous; she has warmth and strength of character; she lives in SE London where she pursues a wide range of hobbies.

Dedicated to Gail, Linda L, Adrian, John Paul, Gary and Steven F, John D for their patience and genius.

Audrey Carnegie

... She Had Wings

AUSTIN MACAULEY PUBLISHERS™

LONDON • CAMBRIDGE • NEW YORK • SHARJAH

A CIP catalogue record for this title is available from the British Library.

ISBN 9781398430358 (Paperback)
ISBN 9781398430365 (ePub e-book)

www.austinmacauley.com

First Published 2022
Austin Macauley Publishers Ltd®
1 Canada Square
Canary Wharf
London
E14 5AA

I would like to acknowledge my coffee loving friends and diners, especially Linda L, Veronica, John Paul, Rose, Laura and Jackie, who apart from the jokes were also very good listeners.

A series of short stories for teenagers, or younger, opening their minds and imaginations and so, encouraging them to look at life and people from different perspectives.

Can You Hear Me

As I walked into the store, there were several shoppers milling around and there stood a young boy, his back against a wall as if he had been pinned there. He was a beautiful looking little boy, aged about 4 or 5 years old and of mixed race. His skin looked so soft you wanted to touch it.

He was so sad, I smiled and waved to him to try and cheer him, by just flicking his wrist he responded, I giggled it was so strange, his face remained stern. I began to wonder what he had done wrong, what was he being punished for? Looking around I saw an older boy perhaps a brother, they have some resemblance. He, the older boy was about 11, he was tall and commanding, dealing with what I assumed was the baby of the group. They were crowded around, whom I assumed to be mother. She had his same dark cool skin and a large afro.

I looked back at the boy still back against the wall and hands by his side, as if waiting to be shot. I smiled again. His eyes shone, I approached the woman, 'excuse me,' I said, "Is that your son pointing to the wall hanger?' 'Yes,' she responded taking more interest in the shelf in front of her. 'Please, can I speak to him?' I said. 'Of course,' she said, not even looking at me.

I approached the boy, 'Hi, you look so sad, why are you sad?' He looked at me stern faced; then looked at his older brother who was hugging the baby. 'So what did he do to you?' I thought to myself. 'Did he reject you or reprimand you? Is that your brother over there?' I asked, following his eyes. He nodded. 'Are you in trouble?' I asked. 'He shouted at me, and Mum didn't listen.' 'Oh ok,' I said, 'Perhaps you need to speak a bit louder.' From his slurred speech, I realised the boy was deaf. Putting my hand in my pocket I produced a small chrome whistle. 'Here,' I said, 'Next time you want to be heard, just tap whoever you want to talk to, if they ignore you, blow softly on this whistle.'

The boy's face lit up into a wonderful smile as he reached out taking the whistle. 'What is your name?' He was about to answer then hesitated and went to his mother and spoke to her, I followed. His mother looked at me 'His name is Harry,' she said, 'I told him not to tell anyone his name.' 'Oh,' I said, 'I have given him a whistle to help him to be heard.' She turned to look at Harry, who was cherishing his whistle. That is a grand idea, especially if we are in a crowd. 'Thank you,' she said. As I started to walk away, I stepped into my wings, the mother looked at Harry then turned to me. 'Thank you,' she said turning and looking around for me and finding an empty space. I waved to Harry, and he waved back smiling at his mother's confusion.

Jeopardy

The boy came rushing down the stairs, he jumped the last few. 'Look out, where are you going in such a rush?' his mother shouted as the door slammed. He was late again, but by chance it meant the bullies would already be in school. Joe drifted along hands in his pockets, he was feeling free and happy, the roads were now part empty after the school rush.

He skipped as he went round a corner, jeopardy, he had walked right into the gang who he thought he had outwitted. They stood in their uniforms puffing on cheap cigarettes. He was suddenly grabbed, and a hand went swiftly over his mouth, 'Money,' the big blond lad, Terry, ordered hand outstretched, he did not argue. His hand then slid into Joe's pocket and out came the £10 note, he had been given for his lunch and bus fare. 'No need to hand it over lad, it's in my hand,' the blond boy said grinning. He had not expected such a big prize. 'OK I will be kind to you today, I won't beat you to the regular pulp,' he turned Joe round and gave him a kick on the backside and the gang wandered off, late for school, that is if they were going. Joe stood watching them go, he had a good walk to school now as he had no bus fare, it was a good long length.

He, as if guided, started walking slowly head down along the High Street and well, he bumped into their neighbour. Who happened to be Terry's mum, 'Joe, you're late for school this morning, Come on I'll drop you off at the school gate on my way to the Town Hall?' Joe thought, double jeopardy. 'Mrs Doughty, please can you come and tell the Receptionist that I lost my wallet and was having to walk?' 'Of course Joe, your mum wouldn't be happy with me if I didn't help,' she said.

Joe smiled, he knew the rigorous Receptionist would report that her son Terry, the blond one was not at school. He would surely get it when he gets home. His dad is a bigger bully and very handy with his fist, the school kids called his dad the bully's bully.

Of course, the Receptionist thanked Mrs Doughty for helping Joe then said, 'And so where is your son?' she paused, 'And his friends,' their teachers have reported them absent.' 'He left home in good time this morning,' Mrs Doughty said looking confused, 'His dad is at home mending the fence, I'll give him a ring and see what he can find out.'

When Terry was presented to the school Receptionist an hour later, he seemed to have had an accident. 'What has happened to you?' the Receptionist asked looking at his swollen lips, his grazed cheek and limp. Terry mumbled that he had run into the gang from the nearby school. The Receptionist advised him to visit the medical room, Terry steadied his rucksack on his shoulder, nodded to his dad then he signed in and headed for his class, as his dad stride out of the school's front door.

On the way to his class, he ran into Joe coming out of the toilet, frightened Joe eyed him and then rushed into his classroom; he had such a big broad smile on his face, his teacher asked him if he had won a prize. His guardian angel looked on also with a smile for she knew that this vulnerable little lad would now be able to walk to school in peace because she knew that the two parents would be chatting, questions would be asked and two would add up with a severe warning put in place.

New School

The Green's, Thomas, Michelle and their daughter Anna had moved to their new house during the school holiday and what a long one it was for Anna to be thinking of a new school.

The new house was great, she had a room of her own and they had their own kitchen and bathroom, not having to share like in the hostel they had just left. The worst thing about the hostel was having to queue every day to use the toilet. Most of the time, it smelt so bad that you'd rushed in and out as quick as you could. Dad had lost his job and as Mum was having a new baby, we could not keep up with the mortgage, so the council moved us to the hostel. We lived in that horrible B and B for seven months, Mum cried every day when Dad went out to look for work.

One day when Mum was praying for a new home, there was a knock at the door. Mum answered to a tall smiling lady, she looked strange to me, so I was staring at her. It was spring but it was still very cold and rainy, yet she had a suntan, that kind of glowed. Her eyes were very blue, she looked warm; she smiled at me, and you had to smile back. The woman told my Mum, 'Do not cry dear, your prayers have been heard.' Who heard Mum's prayers? There were just the two of us and of course the baby we were expecting. 'Are you from the church?' I asked. She responded with a smile, the smile adults give when you should be quiet, she reached into her bag and handed me a book, 'Here's a little present for you,' Go and read that while I talk to your mother. The book seemed to expand; to me , but how did she get the book in that small bag?' The book was so interesting, I'm sure the pictures in it moved and the characters spoke to me funny. As soon as she stopped talking to Mum, I got to the last page. 'Good read,' she said.

'Yes very,' I said.

Mum was looking much happier and when Dad came, I heard them talking about new housing being built outside London. 'We do not have the money to pay the deposit,' Dad said. Mum told him the lady said to keep looking for work and you should carefully check out the organisation's companies along Jenner Drive.

The following morning it was the same old drama. Mum smiling as she saw Dad off and then the mask slipped, and I was left trying to cheer her up. Dad had told Mum that he had an appointment at the Job Centre, they had arranged a couple of interviews and he, after, had to report back to say how he had got on. He promised he would try the restaurants and companies along Jenner Drive on his way home.

When Dad came home in the late evening, as he came through the door, he shouted, 'Just look what I found.' Mum and I rushed to see his find. Dad was holding up an expensive-looking watch. ', That must be worth some serious money,' Mum said, 'You had better take it to the police station. There is probably a reward for that watch whoever lost it, must be very upset.'

Dad looked glum; mum looked at him sternly. Dad shoved the watch in his pocket, 'I will take it in tomorrow.'

Dad sat at the breakfast table the following morning, admiring the watch. 'Let me see Dad,' I said. Dad laid the watch in the palm of my outstretched hand, it throbbed, it was heavy, and the glass case glistened. 'I think it is a magic watch Dad,' I said handing it back.

Dad took the watch to the police station and when he returned home, he informed us that the desk clerk had said that a lady had reported losing it and they would contact her. Dad said they had taken his details and would let him know what happens.

Two days later, Dad received a telephone call to visit the police station to meet the owner of the watch. When Dad returned home, he was so happy. The lady, the owner, said the watch was an heirloom, she had given him a cheque reward for £10,000 and she told him where there was a vacant job. Dad said he thanked her and went straight to see the boss of the firm the lady had recommended. 'What's weird,' Dad said, 'The boss said that one of his workers had left the day before and wanted to know who told me about the job. He gave me a trial and took me on, straight away, I start at 08:30 in the morning.' 'So here I am with a new job,' and Mum butted in, 'And deposit for a new house, there is much to laugh about.' 'Dad,' I said, 'What was the lady like? 'Bit strange,' he said, 'Funny eyes so blue and lovely skin.' 'Was it glowing?' I asked. Dad looked at me oddly, 'Yea kind of.' So here I am thinking about the new school. 'You will be fine,' a voice said. I know it was her.

Uniforms

Uniforms are things that tend to make everyone equal, well almost equal, an example of this is school uniform. There is nothing like watching a class of school children out on an educational trip, all dressed the same but each one has their own character, their own classroom problems and also different home lives.

I sometimes think that mums should wear uniforms when they drop off the children at the school gate in their cars; for some, it's a bravado, 'look at my car', 'my car is the latest', 'oh it's my car, my husband has his own'. Tut! some of those mothers do not have husbands and struggle to make ends meet, but they manage with the help of the uniform to make their child not feel out of place. If the council has given a parent a school uniform grant, or a voucher for free school meals, it no one else's problem in fact, it is a private matter.

Clare came from such a family, but it did not bother her as she was a caring child and watched how her mother struggled to keep her and her sister happy. Clare was 14 years old and her sister, Michelle, 12, who had collected the nick name Mikee. Mum, Jean, was a solid hard-working woman since the death of her husband, Frank. She had kept things going, she had two jobs; she did early morning cleaning leaving home on Mondays to Saturdays morning at 5.00 am to clean nearby offices. In the evenings, she cleaned a primary school, sometimes here she was lucky, she would retrieve items thrown away as useless which the girls made use of. During the days, Jean did repairs for the local dry cleaners and anyone else wanting garments altered.

When the girls came home from school, it was homework first and then they had their own chores to tackle. Frank had been a keen gardener, both girls loved being outdoors and so they took care of the garden; I often helped out correcting and replanting when they were out, shopping, watching Mikee at football training and matches, at the youth club or on occasions a visit to the cinema. When the neighbours and visitors to the house commented on the garden, Jean would proudly point out that Clare was the main gardener. At nights when Jean fell asleep over her sewing, I would complete the work for her, I smiled at times when she woke to start again and finding the work done took herself up to bed feeling she had done the work.

After football training, one afternoon Coach Brown approached Jean informing her that he would like to register Mikee for the team, 'She has got class,' he said, 'She is better than most of the boys.' 'I don't want to stand in her way,' Jean said, 'But how much is it going to cost?' Taking Jean further away from any listening ears, Coach Brown sad 'We know you can't afford to pay all the fees. A kid of her standard should one day play for England. We will have the team fees reduced, so instead of £180.00 for the season, you pay £70.00'. 'Does that include the kit?' Jean asked. 'The parents pay for the kit, when the kids grow out of them, they give them to us. We got a match next Sunday; a strong team and

Mikee is our secret weapon.' 'OK,' Jean said, 'We brought her that kit she is wearing for her birthday last month. Can't she wear that? It's almost the same colour as your kit.' 'That's OK,' Coach Brown said, 'I will tell the other team that her kit didn't come through on time,' he smiled. Jean feeling more at ease said, 'OK but let me have the match details in advance.'

Folding my wings I had decided to go and watch the match. As I wandered to the pitch, I saw Jean standing proudly with Clare on their side of the pitch; on the other side stood all the white families. I approached her, 'I've come to watch the match, I've heard about your daughter which one is she' I said, 'That's my daughter Jean said pointing at Mikee warming up with the team.' The game kicked off with Mikee sitting on the subs bench with three others, she watched the match eagerly following the other team. At half-time Mikee's team, the Bear Cubs were trailing 4-0, the Raiders were in their element, 'that another win,' their striker boasted, 'They can't catch us now.'

At the start of the second half, Mikee took to the pitch with the Raiders laughing, 'She's a girl,' one said. However, Mikee had not been wasting her time on the subs' bench she had weighed up the Raiders and as the whistle blew, she quickly picked up the ball and waded through passing accurately to her players, 4-1, she tackled Raiders' big midfielder nut- megging him and racing on to score, 4-2. Of course, the Raiders started to panic as their striker headed for the goal Mikee tackled him sending the ball over the net of Bear's goal. Bear's goalie kicked the ball into midfield, it bounced twice, Mikee was quick on it before the second bounce heading the ball into the net, 4-3. In a hurry to up the score, the Raiders defender scored a home goal 4-4; hurt by his team's anger, he reverted to tears and was replaced by a sturdy-looking lad, it seemed he had been instructed to mark Mikee. However, when Mikee took off, he was left standing. Bears' striker was tackled badly and had to be replaced. Mikee and Jake smiled they had discussed tactics while sitting on the sub bench. Soon it was 4-5 as the game got heated, Jake lobed a ball to a running Mikee who stuck it in the goal, 4-6.

Coach Brown approached Jean, 'See what did I told you? That girl will play for England one day,' , 'Incidentally the Raiders were unbeaten last season and what did their striker say, she's a girl he said'. He moved back to the bench with the sound of his players cheering as they had scored goal number 7. Raider's goalie kicked a ball out but not far enough Mikee struck it back into his goal ending the match 4-8.

After the game, a few of the parents from Raiders approached Coach Brown, 'That girl was not playing in proper kit, is that legit and how old is she? she's too strong to be playing for this age group.' Coach Brown beckoned to Raiders manager and then from his case, he went back to the parent, 'Her kit didn't get delivered in time and as for her age, here is her registration; your manager gave her permission to play in her own kit,' Looking at their manager's disappointment, a parent said 'oops' and they dispersed.

That match took place seven years ago and having gone through The Bear Cubs to the Bears Women's Football Club, creating havoc with their winning streak at 16 years old Mikee was playing for the England U16s, she was occasionally selected to play for the England Women, if there were injures. Mikee is now a paid player, and her match fees adds to the home's pot. Coach Brown, who is now a good family friend, who helps out with repairs. I sometimes cause a little upset which means that often Coach Brown transports Jean, Clare and I, unknowingly, to watch Mikee play. They will be a family one day. Mikee's kit has become her uniform.

Brothers

He was such a sad little boy, although he was playing with the other children, his heart was not there. Somehow, he seemed distant from the others whilst their eyes were sparkling with excitement, his were dull. His brother came bounding over and knocking him to the ground and started to punch him, anyone looking on would have thought they were play fighting, but he was a mean spiteful child, his mother's favourite, the cutie whilst his brother was deep and shy. As suddenly as he'd rushed over, he'd gone again, the brother not getting a chance to hit back, not that he would. John, that's his name, sat on the ground rubbing his arm. 'I wish he would leave me alone,' he said to himself.

'You need a cuddle from your grandma,' I said willing her to come over, she rushed up to him arms open for him to rush into. 'What are you doing here on your own?' she asked. 'I fell over,' he said, 'let's go and get some marshmallows and lemonade,' she said. Looking across the room, John's brother Clive was sitting on his mother's lap, his arms wrapped tightly around her neck. Did she not have enough love for both her children? I summoned his dad who came clutching his glass of beer, 'Hi son,' he said, 'How are you doing?' John quickly pushed his small hand into his father's. Here was a child who

23

needed to belong, to feel loved. Transferring my thoughts John, I said, he looked at me 'How about we go and have a chat', 'I want to stay with my daddy, and I don't know you' john said. I would like to get to know you and I mean you no harm, ' I said, 'If you look into my eyes, you can see I am really a new friend.' John looked at me and, in that time, I held his gaze unfolded my wings and told him I want to help him as I walked towards a bench. John looked up at his dad, 'I'm going to sit on that bench with that lady,' he said to his dad. 'What lady?' his dad asked, only John could see me. 'Oh, OK,' his dad said humouring John, tell 'the lady I said hello'. John my name is Daphne, I am your guardian angel only you can see and hear me. I am here to help you and you only; I have come to see you because you are not having a good time. I am going to help you to be happy, let us go and play with the other children, do not tell them about me.

The children were playing happily together. Clive came over shouting and rushing towards John. I suddenly steered John out of the way leaving Clive to fall flat on his face. The other children laughed at him and gathered around John, 'Boy, John, you sure dumped him,' they shouted. 'Tell them you've been practicing,' I whispered. 'I have been practicing,' John said leaning down to help Clive up. They all ran off to play, Clive with a face like thunder told himself John did not win. Back home Clive and John were in their rooms doing their homework. John was working diligently, while Clive relied on his mum to help him. Homework was done, they both had a snack and story before heading for bed. Whilst John slept, Clive crept into his room and tore out the pages of his homework. He screwed the pages up and threw them in the bin. I fished them out and running my fingers down the pages un-creased it, then holding the pages to the book and blowing on it I resealed the pages; closing the book I placed it in John's school bag.

In the morning when the boys were ready for school, Clive was very jovial, it's hard sometimes to try and explain how siblings can suffer from jealousy. Clive was cute, curly-haired, quick-witted with a ready smile which he used to charm people. John was serene, shy and intelligent. He did not, however, show his full potential. He lacked confidence so Clive got the 'oohs' and 'aahs'.

At school, Clive was gleefully telling his friend Richie, another mean sibling, how he had destroyed John's homework. He was, therefore, very confused at playtime when he saw John's class entering the playground, the other children were cheering John on getting a whole 10/10, the highest mark, for his homework. Clive's friend Richie looked at him scornfully, 'You little fibber! Anyway, why are you so mean to your brother?' he said walking away. One of john's classmates approached Clive, 'So you're not the brain of the family then,' he said. Clive sheepishly threw his arms around his brother and said, 'Good on you, John.'

Back at home, Clive sneaked into John's room. He searched the bin but could not find the page he had torn out. 'Show me your homework John,' he said. Clive's eyes widened as the pages he had destroyed looked back at him. He couldn't say nothing or tell anyone how mean he had been, he was sure he had definitely torn the pages out.

John's confidence was building, people were now giving him time, he was more verbal and learnt to say 'no' to Clive and mean it. His final glory came on sports day when his goal won his class the Sports Day trophy. John found his voice, grew in confidence, found love and friendship in his brother who had to learn how to share in all things, which included their mother.

Brown Eyes

She had beautiful eyes that seemed to follow you around a room, this unruly child was running around the front and joining room touching everything. The carer's eyes followed her, perhaps thinking do I want such an unruly child in my house. The social worker was gleefully chattering away, another placement had gone, unaware just glad to get rid of her charge.

As the social worker left the house, the carer called the child, 'let's have a little chat, this is not where you run about, there is a garden and also those things,' she said pointing to some ornaments, 'Are very precious to me so please do not touch them.' The child looked at her with her big brown eyes, now wide in anticipation, what next. 'Come let's have a look around now,' she said taking the child's hand and leading her upstairs. 'This is your room.' 'You mean I have a room of my own, my chair, my wardrobe?' 'Yes, it's all yours,' the Carer said, stroking the child's hair. 'Oh my God I'm in heaven,' I smiled. 'Are you my new mum?' the child looked up with her pleading big brown eyes. 'No darling, you can call me Auntie,' 'but can you be my pretend mum then? The child said 'Why?' asked the carer. 'It's funny you kind of remind me of my mum. She always liked holding my hand and your hand is as soft as hers.' 'Of course, if you want, but remember your mum is in heaven and she is very special.'

'Tomorrow we will go shopping and get some nice new clothes because you did not come with much; come on here is the bathroom, there is another toilet next door but it's better for you to use this one, it's lower. That is my room and that one is our spare room.' Squeezing the Carer's hand, the child asked again, 'Can I call you Mum?' 'No darling, your Mum is in heaven watching over you, come and see the garden. Then let us go and have a snack.'

Whilst the carer was in the kitchen making their snack, the child wandered all around the house, she looked at all the special ornaments that she was not to touch. She popped her head around the kitchen door 'why are the ornaments special? she asked, 'They are a reminder of my other children.'

As she looked at them, the child thought what other children -, looking around and noting the Carer was not about, she was about to pick up a small round colourful paperweight, pulling her hand back she told herself it will always be there for her to look at. She went into her room, sat on the bed and using her feet bounced off the floor, she laid on it and cuddled the pillows, she spread her whole body over the bed, before she had had to share a bed much smaller. She heard her name being called and headed for the kitchen, she looked up at the carer and said, 'Thank you, I am home'.

The child's mother smiled with her daughter's guardian angel witnessing and seeing that her mischievous daughter had been happily grounded without threats and tears would be cared for by an earth angel.

Carl

I hovered outside the house; it was a house that was shouting for help. Walking up the drive I rang the doorbell, I was aware she, the mother, could see me standing on her doorstep. She took a long time answering, I was just about to walk away when the door flung open, she looked at me quizzingly then said, 'Come in, I am just about to feed Carl.' Now if you did not know Carl has physical disabilities that means he is a disabled young boy. He was lying on his day bed; he was 10 years old. Balancing him half in her lap and the day bed the mother proceeded to feed her child with milk.

She was a prisoner in her own home, her break was the three hours frame whilst he was at school, where she did the shopping, the housework, kept appointments etc whilst her husband was at work.

It was good to visit. We would chat about the garden, the people who irked her. 'I cannot understand why they are so horrible to me,' she said. 'There are some that are envious of you, jealous because you are such a nice person and they know nothing about you, they lack courage because of your beauty. What some people do not understand they are afraid of.' 'How can they envy me?' she said. 'You have a beautiful child, a good home full of love, you have a beautiful soul,' I said. 'But hardly anyone speaks to me when we are out,' she said looking deeply at me. 'Your child is beautiful, his disabilities are something they don't understand, As I said what people do not understand. They fear. How would you feel if a someone stopped you in the street and started asking you about your child, there are medical questions that you yourself cannot and do not want to answer, would that give you confidence or make you think that they are just prying? Why don't you make yourself a cup of tea while I have a chat with Carl?' There were tears in her eyes, 'They fear they will upset you; they don't know what to say,' I called after her, 'But they are not all like that, in time, a few will begin to understand.'

I walked over and took the boy's hand. He turned his head and smiled at me, then looked at his mother; he again looked deeply at me, his thoughts transferring to me. 'I am very lucky,' he said, 'My parents adore me, they have to do everything for me. what other people cannot see is that I am just another child.' 'Carl, you are such a beautiful child you have what a lot of children are aching for, loving parents who will care so much about them.' 'Your father is your feet, he carries you where you need to go, look at your clothes both he and your mum make sure your every need is met, that is love. When you and I are alone we have so many things to talk about,' Carl smiled. 'I love the stories you tell me, 'He giggled. His mother looked at me and said, 'he is so happy when you visit.'

Carl said, 'I am in a body that restricts me, but I am happy'. 'I know you are' I said sending the thoughts back. 'You are a very special child.' 'Wrap your wings around my mum and give her some love from me,' he said. 'So you know who I am then?' I spoke. 'Yes,' he said, 'From the day I came home, you have always been here looking after us. Your wings are beautiful they shimmer when you have wrapped them around my mum and dad when they are upset. You have such bright blue eyes; they are so caring and peaceful. Mum talks to me a lot but please keep visiting, she needs someone to answer back.'

'Would you like a drink?' Mother said, 'No thanks, I shall have to go now just called for our regular chat.' 'Oh come and visit again soon,' she said. Carl turned his head, 'Yes please because I can talk to only you, goodbye angel.'

My Nan

'Still raw and rejected from the divorce. Rogue! He got everything. What have I ended up with? Our daughter, an 8year-old and a high-rise 3 floored council flat. Weeks later, I'm still trying to rid the smell of tobacco and dope, yellowish walls-streaked grease marks. Those useless council officials! If I was an illegal, they wouldn't have stuck a mother and child in an ex-drug den.' The doorbell rang disrupting her anger. 'Mum, someone at the door,' daughter Keisha yelled. 'I'm not deaf,' mother said looking into the daughter's room as she headed for the door. 'Get away from that window it's not safe.' 'What's wrong with it?' Keisha asked. 'Who knows,' her mother retorted, 'The whole place is a disaster.'

Opening the door, her ex-husband stuck his foot in the doorway anticipating her slamming it in his face. He stood holding a box of chocolates, he sneered, 'No they are not for you.' 'Keisha,' he yelled. Keisha came out of her room rushed into his arms; 'Keisha go to your room', mother shouted. 'Oh no Mum not again,' she shouted, grabbing the chocolates, ran into her room and slammed the door.

Her parents were arguing that's all they ever did. She thought, 'It's always about me, they don't want me. Oh I wish my Nan was here,' tears were now streaming down her cheeks, angrily she stuck her head out of her bedroom. 'Why don't you two grow up? I'm the child,' she slammed the bedroom door again. Keisha went over to the window, she could see the trees gently shedding their leaves, now and then leaves slammed against the window pane. Through the branches, looking down, cars were driving past, people standing at a bus stop in the distance. Children playing on the green. Suddenly, there she was, 'That's my Nan, there's my Nan,' Keisha shouted leaning closer against the window excitedly, there was a creaking sound, then the sound of something cracking as the window gave way, 'Mum, Dad,' she shouted, her shouts were drowned in their argument.

Floating down towards the green, she thought: 'I'm going to die, no one cares.' Suddenly she felt as though she was being carried in someone's arms. Opening her eyes, she looked into her Nan's face, 'Nan, I love you so much,' Keisha said as she lost consciousness. People rushed towards her; the sound of an ambulance could be heard; her parent was summoned each blaming the other.

At the hospital, the consultant paced the floor, 'This child fell from a 3rd floor window; she does not have one broken bone or a bruise.' As he spoke, Keisha's eyes opened, 'Where is my Nan?' she asked. The consultant sent his junior to the parents. Returning white-faced, the junior consultant, looking at the consultant said, 'The parents say her Nan died 4 years ago, Sir.'

Alone Keisha shifted in her bed, she asked, 'Nan, why did you leave me?' Her Nan responded, 'I never left you darling but that's our secret.' Nan said winking at the child's guardian angel.

Black

It was a warm sunny day in August, the school holidays, my mum took me to the park. We were in the enclosed area with other young people playing on the swings and other equipment. I noticed a group of children playing rounders, I stood watching, my mum said, 'Why don't you ask them if you can play?' she watched me as I made my way to the group. 'Please can I play?' I asked. The boy holding the bat looked at me and sneered, 'NO.' 'Why?' I asked. 'Because you're black,' he retorted before continuing to try and hit the ball. OK, I thought to myself: 'So I'm black that doesn't mean I can't hit the ball.'

Mum was still watching from the enclosure. I didn't want her to know I was upset so I sat on the grass near the group. I heard someone say, 'So you're black, are you going to let that bother you?' Looking behind me I saw a woman, she looked a bit strange, she had funny eyes, they were blue and seemed to look through me, she had beautiful skin though it was tanned and glowing. I said, 'I'm not going to cry.' She said, 'If you sit here long enough, they will let you play, good for you.' 'They are not very good anyway,' I said.

The boy who had shouted at me started to have an argument with a girl in his team. 'You can't even hit the ball;

girls are useless,' he shouted. The girl got upset and tried again to hit the ball. 'Ha ha,' he laughed. The girl fed up with the bully, threw the bat down and stomped out of the enclosure sitting on the grass she sat eying him angrily. 'Nah, nah, now you do not have a team,' shouted a girl from the other team, 'We win.' The bully looking around seeing no one else said, 'Ok blackie, you can play.' The glittery lady said, 'Tell him your name.' I found myself saying, 'My name is Sarah not Blackie, do you not have any manners?' The bully looked at his shoes, the others were waiting, he looked again, 'Ok sorry, my name is Jason.' I joined his team and although I had never played before, I was hitting the ball far and wide. It was as if someone was guiding the ball to the bat.

I was very excited when I joined my mum, 'Did you see that?' I said, 'I scored all the runs, did you hear them shouting my name? That boy,' I said pointing to Jason, said 'They always play here, and I should come and join his team.' Mum was pleased for me; she knew I did not have many friends and that a door had been opened. As the children were leaving the park with their parents, they turned and waved to me. The mums were also waving and so Mum and I waved back.

I turned to mum, 'Did you see the lady that was sitting with me? You know I have never seen anyone with such bright blue eyes. She told me that it does not matter who you are, you must always stand up for yourself so other people know you are there.' Mum said, 'But Sarah you were sitting on your own, waiting your turn.' 'But Mum,' I said staring ahead as I saw the lady coming towards us. As she passed us, she had a finger to her lips. She winked at me as she passed, I turned to see a large pair of wings and she was gone. Mum said, 'Perhaps, we sometimes feel we need a friend and imagine one.' 'But it was so real,' I said pinching myself.

Labels Go to The Back

Sometimes at nurseries, you can tell how well a child has been taught to look after themselves, or the little things parents don't think of. There are the little boys who had to be taught to stand over a bowl to wee; oh, the fun they have after often missing the targets. When the mothers complain about mopping the floor, we just say, 'But they are boys, their targets will get better.'

With little girls, it's the case of knickers being back to front. We advise mums until they get older to buy knickers with pictures on the front. We then have the mums who refuse to let their children grow up, they turn up not potty trained, can't do up a button, crying at the touch of a feather, a few arriving at school in a pushchair - some mums definitely need parental training. For the first day, they leave in tears, while the child has gone off to play not even saying goodbye, perhaps the child sees it as an escape.

However, one day a very confused little boy came to the nursery, he was not connecting, he played on his own or sat quietly looking at the other children. His Nan brought and collected him, she spoke no English and grunted instructions to him. The nursery workers tried to integrate him, spent time with him, but there was no interest.

I was to be his friend, his guide, I became a little girl again. As he sat at a table trying to do a jigsaw, I sat at his table. I said nothing, he looked at me. I did not meet his gaze. I kept looking at the pieces of the puzzle. When one piece of the puzzle fell on the floor, I picked it up replacing it on the table and walked away. He watched me as I sat at an empty table. This went on for a few days, in his mind, I was as lonely as he was.

He was dyslectic he slurred, he, Raymond, often came to the nursery with his clothes in disarray, often his jumper or T-shirt was back to front; he sometimes walked funny because quite often his pants were also back to front and rubbing, chaffing his leg. The boys would run out of the toilet shouting Raymond has got his pants back to front. Poor Raymond would come out of the toilet looking like a mess. One of the nursery workers would take Raymond into a cubicle and sort him out. One day, as the other children teased him, Raymond started to cry. I put my arms around him and whispered, 'The label goes to the back.' He looked at me in surprise, 'It was the first time I had spoken to him.' He repeated, 'The label goes to the back,' Raymond smiled. I went to my empty table, Raymond came and sat next to me. We played with the Lego together.

When Raymond came to nursery the following day, his clothes were on the right way around. He smiled at me and said, 'The label goes to the back, right?' 'Yea,' I said. 'Will you be my friend?' he slurred. I said' 'Yes, let us play sounds.' Before long, Raymond's words were unravelling, and he was mixing with the other children. The other children could now understand his words and they had nothing to tease him about. I told Raymond that we were moving to a new house, and I was leaving. Raymond threw his arms around me, 'I'll miss you,' he said, 'You were my first friend. I will always remember you, you're so blue eyes and the funny feeling I got when you held my hand 'do you believe in angels?', he asked, 'why I asked. 'Because my Nan said you're a little angel, because I'm OK now and I've got lots of friends'. 'I will miss you too Raymond' I said as I walked away.

Reject

The child was sobbing into her pillow, it had been the same for a few weeks. I sat on her bed and lulled her to sleep. Morning came and she got up, dressed herself, she then went to the bathroom took her flannel and running it under the cold tap, wiped her face; she brushed her teeth with a worn-out toothbrush. Hair uncombed, she went into the kitchen, took a slice of bread and plastered it with margarine. Breakfast done, she knocked on her mother's bedroom door and shouting through the closed door, 'I'm off to school now,' she listened for a response, none came.

She joined a group of parents taking their children to school, crossing the road with them but once at the school gate, she became a solitary child, invisible, playing on her own. I joined her, 'Hello Hannah,' I said. She was startled 'You know my name?' she said, 'Are you a friend of my Mum?' 'No,' I said, 'I've come to be your special friend.' She lifted her head to look at me, 'That will be nice,' she said shielding her eyes from the sun as she looked at me.

'Tell me about yourself,' I said. 'Well, I am 6 years old; I live with my mum, she is always busy or cross with me, I do try to be good and not bother her.' 'So where is Dad?' I asked. 'I do not know,' Hannah said, 'He has been gone for a very long time, I do not remember him much,' she burst into tears, 'He used to love me.' I hugged her, 'He still does, darling,' I said. The bell was ringing, 'Hannah, I'll be here for you when school is over,' I said

I noted a teacher stretching her hand out to Hannah, which she clutched turning to me, she waved and was gone. Wrapping my wings around me, I followed them into the classroom, here Hannah had found a place amongst the children. She joined in with the activities, answering questions and generally laughing at learning. Morning playtime, the same teacher took Hannah into the staff cloakroom, she washed her, changed her clothes from a stock of worn uniforms in a cupboard and combed her hair as if it was a routine. Mother didn't care as long as she had a bottle of rum or whisky.

I met up with Hannah after school and we walked to McDonalds, 'Is it my birthday?' she asked. 'No,' I said, 'This is our secret, what would you be having at home?' I asked. 'Bread, if there is any left,' she said sadly.

For the next week whilst Hannah slept, I hunted for her father on our 'cloud computer'. He was called Craig, mother had thrown him out when Hannah was 3, he had refused to keep her supplied with booze, to spite him, she held onto Hannah denying him any contact

Craig had given up after years battling for contact, he now had a new wife, Maria, and a red setter which they both adored but no children. A photograph of a young-looking Hannah had pride of place on a cupboard.

I waited until Craig's wife had left for work, knocking at the door, he answered with, 'Ok so what have you forgotten,' with a smile on his face. The smile changed when he saw me,

41

'Can I have a word about your daughter?' I spoke. He practically dragged me inside. I informed Craig that Hannah needed him and advised him on how to get custody of her. He listened earnestly 'Maria and I will have often wandered how she was getting on' . After I had left within 15 minutes, Craig left the house. I followed him to a solicitor's office in High Street and wrapping my wings, I listened and prompted their mind thoughts until the paperwork was done. 'I want her as soon as possible,' Craig said. 'With this information, the Court will not argue,' the solicitor said.

Two weeks later as Hannah and I walked to school, I said, 'There is a surprise after school.' 'Is my mum coming to pick me up? She has not done so for ages.' 'We will see,' I said.

As Hannah entered the school, the teacher approached me, 'Have you heard,' she said excitedly, 'Hannah's father has been found, we are so happy for her.' 'That is good news,' I said.

After school, Craig stood proudly in the playground waiting for his daughter, 'Will she remember me?' he said anxiously clutching a new doll. 'Of course, she will,' I said. 'She is so lucky to have you as a care for her .' My wife said, 'You must be an angel since you arrived, everything has gone well, and we now have a daughter.' I smiled, Craig looked at me, 'Gosh I never noticed before, you have such beautiful blue eyes.' I smiled said 'goodbye' and moved away.

Hannah came out of the door walking towards me as she peered at Craig, I shifted his age backwards, their eye met reflecting recognition, she stood, took a step forward, 'Daddy,' she queried, then rushing into his arms, 'Oh Daddy, where have you been?' she shouted. Craig gathered her into his arms, 'Looking for you my princess and I have found you at long last.' Hannah looked at me, 'It's my dad, it's my dad, can we go to McDonalds with my friend?' she asked her dad. 'What friend?' Dad asked. 'She over there' Craig turned to look, he stood staring at me. I beckoned to Hannah whilst her dad spoke to her teacher, 'you have a new life now and I know you will be happy,' before walking away. Craig still staring at his daughter walked towards her. Hannah turned to wave goodbye but saw no one, 'Where did she go Dad?' she asked. ' Who love,' he said. Dad, my friend the lady you came with she has beautiful blue eyes that sparkled and made me happy. Craig looked up to the sky and said 'thank you' under his breath, he recalled she did have such blue eyes.

Why, I Don't Understand

'I don't understand,' he said looking at me as we sat discussing his role in the household. He was not new as this was his second foster home; he had been living there for several weeks he had also been thrown out of his last college was starting at another.

'Why', she asked. 'I don't know,' he said. I smiled. It's strange how age can be used as a barrier for ignorance. 'So,' she said, 'You will tidy your room each morning on early college days. Wednesday evening, you will do your washing and do the vacuuming.' 'I am only cleaning up what I use,' he said. 'You live in our household you will help to keep it clean,' she said. He looked at her and realised she was serious, 'Oh,' he said, 'Why should I?' 'Because you live here,' she said. He did not respond.

When he cooked himself a meal that evening, he ignored the washing up, he washed only the plate, knife and fork that he had used. The following day, the cooking utensils that he had used, the pots, frying pan were left on the side of the draining board. He took out different pots and as usual, only washed his plate. She said as he went to enter the kitchen the following day, 'I don't think you are allowed in there; you don't comply.' He, without looking at her, turned and went back to his room but hunger got the better of him. 'I'm hungry,' he said. 'The washing up needs to be done', he went into the kitchen, slamming the door as he did so. I watched as he did the washing up, cooked his meal, ate and washed up after himself.

The following day as he left for college, I accidentally on purpose bumped into him, 'Ha, watch where you are going,' he shouted. I stood my ground looking him straight in the eye, 'What's your problem? Where are your manners?' He was taken aback staring at me open-mouthed, 'Whoa lady you are hot,' he said quietly. 'I had a pretty bad day yesterday, I want to start this one good,' he said. 'So what happened? Speak.' He took a step back, 'I'm in care and the woman keeps harassing me, tidy your room, do this, do that, clean the bath, tidy your mess in the kitchen.' I butted in, 'Oh so you don't like the laws of living, you live in a house you help to keep it clean; would you rather live in a dirty house, would you get into a dirty bath?' 'No but' he started to say, I butted in, 'No but about it, you are an unclean,' 'No I'm not,' he protested. I looked him up and down, 'Then why are your clothes not ironed; you don't smell too good either.' He bit his lip, 'I just wanted to show her I have a mind of my own,' he said. I responded, 'What you showed that carer is your ignorance, it's you who is a smelly unwashed mess.'

I watched as he took it all in seeing himself for what he had become. 'Why are you in care?' I asked. 'Bad behaviour,' he said sulkily. 'Do you not realise how much your mother loves you? She is alone, she works for you, feeds and clothes you, she has put a roof over your head, and you abuse her because she can't give you what she does not have; fancy trainers, designer labels, boy, love is more important.' Tears were rolling down his cheeks, 'I guess I never looked at things that way before,' he said. 'How old are you?' I asked, 'I'm 16,' he said, 'In a few years,' I said, 'You may be where your mother is.' He used his hands to wipe away his tears, 'No one has ever explained thing to me before, why?' he asked. 'It all depends on who is watching,' I replied.

'Miss,' he said, 'Can I ask a favour please?' 'Of course,' I said, 'Please can I borrow a fever, if you give me your address, I will pay you back.' 'What's the money for,' I asked. 'I need to buy my Mum some flowers, I need to go home.' 'You can do me a favour for the money, go and apologise to your carer and tidy yourself up before you visit your mother.' He nodded as he sobbed. He told his carer of his run-in with a strange lady who had told him off, no he said she put me right. I'm so sorry I have been so selfish to you and Mum; can I go and visit her'? The carer hugged him and said 'I'm sure your Mum would love to see you, that lady must have been an angel for you to take notice.

Hours later, I watched as he handed his mother a bunch of flowers, a huge hug with both in tears. 'I'm so sorry Mum, can I come back home now?' he sobbed. Hugging him, she said, 'Your room is still there.' Two weeks later, he was saying goodbye to his Carer and walking away with his mother.

The Earnest Footballer

It was the start of the new football season most of the teams had completed their registration, new kits organised - most of them new. The big excitement for most children is to be selected for that first game, being the first to wear their new kit and the glory if they scored; the comradeship, cheers and hugs.

It's funny with children during the week when parents are rushing them to get up and get ready for school on time, everything is done in slow motion. School books, homework and uniform are strewn around the bedroom. That is Mum's task to find and tidy up. Come Saturday, its football training, it is Dad's turn.

Timothy crept into his parent's room, his mum and dad were deep in sleep, He nudged his dad, gently at first with no response he pulled at him whispering in his ears, 'Come on get up I am going to be late for training, if I get there late, Coach won't let me play tomorrow; I've got my stuff ready and I'm dressed.' Timothy's dad sat up in the bed, 'Tim, training is at 11:30 it barely 8:30, do me a favour and go back to your bed, his mother pipped in, 'I'll make sure you are not late'.

Timothy wandered out of their room agitated, he had got up, he thought I have been good, I washed and put his training clothes on. He sat on the stairs hugging his knees, then hands under his chin, he suddenly looked up towards his younger brother's room. 'I will make sure that they get up,' he said to himself. He crept into Simon's room; Simon was fast asleep with his thumb stuck in his mouth. Timothy stood observing him, 'I hate you,' he told Simon grudgingly, everyone thinks you are so cute.' He pulled Simon's thumb from his mouth, Simon stirred, he ruffled his hair, stuck a finger in his ear. No response. Simon slept on to Timothy's annoyance. Timothy checked his escape route then pinched Simon hard on his left ear, as Simon screamed, he rushed into his room. Mum came rushing into Simon's room, 'Oh darling, what's up?' she said scooping him up, she swayed and hugged him lulling him back to sleep. Laying him back into his cot she went back to bed.

Timothy crept back into Simon's room mimicking his mother, 'Oh darling,' he pinched Simon on his exposed right thigh, then again made his escape. Mum rushed in again, 'Oh Si, I'm so tired I can't keep getting up,' she said as she carried the crying Simon into their bed. Timothy threw himself onto his bed in anger.

At 10 o'clock, his dad got up, he staggered into the bathroom, washed and cleaned his teeth. 'Tim,' he shouted, 'Have you had washed?' 'Yes Dad,' Tim said. 'So Tim, why is your flannel as dry as a bone and the toothpaste?' 'But it's Saturday Dad,' he answered, 'I just used water.' 'Bathroom lad,' his dad shouted and make it smart; Simon has been up twice; you mother is very tired, so you got me to contend with.' 'Dad, are we going to be late then?' Tim asked earnestly. 'Tim my lad, that is up to you,' his dad said, 'I won't get picked for tomorrow if I'm late,' he pleaded.

Mum came downstairs carrying Simon, she put him in his high chair and pushed it to the table, leaving him with a trainer cup of milk; Dad was preparing breakfast in the kitchen, 'I'll sort Simon,' she said. Tim sat glaring at Simon, then it's as if he heard Simon say, 'Why do you keep pinching me?' Simon sat staring back at him, Tim smiled, he can't talk he poked his tongue out at Simon. Simon eyed Tim then aimed his part-filled drinking cup at Tim, it connected over Tim's right eye with the contents spilling down his clothes. Tim wailed in pain, both parents rushed from the kitchen to see Simon giggling and Tim rubbing his forehead. 'He hit me with his cup,' Tim yelled, 'Oh Tim,' Mum said, 'Don't be such a baby, go and change your clothes. Back in the kitchen.' Dad was scraping the burnt toast. 'That will teach you and you're not playing tomorrow.' Tim was sure he heard Simon say as he went out the door.

The family rushed off to the park where Tim rushed off to join his team, the mothers sat whilst their toddlers played, the dads hung around watching their sons. After training the players lined up for selection for the match. One of the Coaches walked Tim to his parents. 'Sorry,' he said, 'The manager said he can't play tomorrow, that eye does not look good, and it could get wore overnight.' Tim stood with the tears rolling down his face, he glared at Simon who was sitting next to a mum who looked like she had wings. 'I'll give him such a pinch,' he thought to himself as he walked towards Simon. 'Timothy,' the winged mum said, 'It's time to stop pinching your brother, he is only a toddler. Why are you making him afraid of you? When he is old enough, he will tell your parents and then what?' Tim turned to look at his parents then turning back to look at them . The lady with the wings was walking away, she turned and said, 'Be good next week, you may make the team.'

Confused

The teenager sat on the chair in the meeting just being difficult, it had to be his way or nothing. He, Billy, had a good home with his parents, a younger sister and at times a foster child over the weekends. He recently had joined a new group of friends but sometimes when friends are poking fun at you, you laugh with them because they are your friends, and you believe everything they tell you. Alan had told him that if he got himself in a care, like him, he could do whatever he wanted. He did not even have to go to college as there was no one to check; Billy's mind was racing thinking about the parties he could attend. However, what Billy did not know was, it was not all fun, they nicked stuff from shops, the older boy sold them on they even picked a few pockets. The lads had the latest clothes and were always talking about parties they had been to.

When he left them in the evenings to get his bus home, he didn't hear them laughing at him, they had found a stooge, away from his parents he would rely on them, he would be of use he was a loner.

'I don't want to be here,' Billy said. I looked at him, 'You are so spoiled and gullible,' I thought, 'You don't even realise how lucky you are, you have a home and all the comforts.'

'So what is wrong with this place?' the social worker asked. 'I want a key; I want to cook my own meals.' 'And you want to take over this house that is not yours?' the social worker should point that out, what about the mortgage, the gas, the electricity and all the other bills; ooh and let's not forget about your food and clothes. Billy was now sulking, he knew he was not telling the truth, so he never once looked at his parents or the social worker during the meeting.

'You don't communicate,' his dad said, 'You spend all your time in your room on your mobile or game box , you answer everything in a little sentence.' 'How are we to know what you want, or your true needs?' his fatigued looking mother said. I moved to his right side and blew in his ear, he raised his hand touching the lobe, I then blew in his other ear, 'Are you listening?' he looked at the social worker who continued, 'You are cared for, you are loved, think about where you are, it's your home, it's a good home, you are not having to share your room, you have freedom'. He thought about the parties and staying out late with his mates, 'I am 16, why should I listen to them?' he thought as he glanced at his parents.

'What do you like doing?' the social worker asked trying to gain his interest, his mind was blank, he then looked at the worried social worker who not wanting to show her displeasure, said 'Maybe we need to re-look at things in another meeting, bringing it to a closure.' 'Why do I have to wait, I want to go now, and I mean now,' Billy shouted. 'Listen son,' his dad said, 'We've done everything for you if we are not good enough, go.' His mother looked at the boy pleadingly. There was no response. The social worker said, 'I'm just stepping out to make a phone call. She returned and stated that there was a vacancy in a nearby Unit, which would suit, and he could move the following day. Billy was in his element.'

As he slept that night, I gently let him into a dream where I carried him into the home of a troubled family, he watched as the family argue over their meagre things, there was so little food, the house was dirty and smelt of stale smoke and dirty feet; from a teenager's room loud music was blaring out. The boy shifted uneasily in his sleep.

Waking hours later he ran his hand over the clean bedding, run his hand over the wallpaper and dug his feet into the carpet. He opened his bedroom door, there was no noise, a radio programme was commenting on the government's latest argument, there were the gentle voices of the other family members.

The social worker arrived the following day, the family watched as he carried his cases to her car, 'Are you sure Billy?' his mother asked. He nodded. Billy did not look back as the car drove off. The social worker took the boy to a Unit, where he was greeted by two of its workers, whilst one of the workers showed the boy his room and discussed the rules of the Unit, the other worker discussed him with the social worker. I watched Billy as he sat on the small single bed, in a small room, the walls were plain, there was no carpet or rug on the floor. In a corner stood a small wardrobe next to which a small chest of draws, his mind flashed to his dream. The Unit worker showed him around, the bathroom, the kitchen, the sitting room, 'You are not allowed in the office visitors are not allowed in your room,' he said concluding his tour. 'Do you know how to get to college from here?' he was asked, Bill, shook his head. The Admin Worker will sort you out a bus pass and give you the route details go to the office so he can take your photo for the pass, he will need your mobile phone number, Billy did as he was told. He later sat in his room reading the rules, he had to be in before 10 p.m. At home, he came home much later, he had to do his own washing and ironing, his mother usually did that, he had to cook his own meals and do his own shopping and he had to clean his room and help with the Unit.

He rang Alan, who told him he was in college and would ring him later, no call came. Alan rang him early Saturday morning asking if he wanted to go shopping with him and the boys. 'Of course,' he said. Billy met up with the group and was instructed to carry a large shopping bag. As he followed them around the shop, he realised that the boys were occasionally dropping things in the bag that were not paid for. He panicked, 'I am not a thief,' he told himself. Billy told Alan he did not want to carry the bag. Alan jabbed him in the ribs and said, 'Yes you will.' From the grocer , they headed for the sports shop, then the music shop where again items were being dropped into the bag.

After the shopping, the boys went to a local park where they sorted their cache. When Billy protested, they informed him that bag carrying was his job in the gang. 'If you get caught, we do not know you, understand! You are in care now.' Like us. Come and see where we live.' He followed them to a run-down looking building, on entering, they had to sign in, including him giving the details to their Admin Worker. We are going shopping tomorrow up West, we will meet you at the train station at 10:30 a.m.,' Alan said threateningly.

Billy made his way back to his Unit, he sat on his bed considering his day, 'What if he had got caught?' his thoughts were interrupted by a girl's voice shrieking loudly, mimicking a pop song. He looked round him then, to get away from the noise he went into the garden. As he sat on a bench looking at the sky, I joined him. 'How has your days been?' I asked. He looked at me in a pleading manner, 'Not a day I want to remember,' Billy said. 'Why?' I asked, 'Were you not with your friends?' 'Some friends,' he said, 'I thought they were friends, they are liars and thieves. I wanted to be with them because they made everything seem fun.' 'Perhaps you just need to meet better friends,' I said. 'Miss,' he said, looking at me strangely, 'I have never been good at making friends.' 'Perhaps you just need a little bit of help,' I said. 'Tomorrow, I can show you where there is a youth club.' 'I'm supposed to meet them tomorrow, I am worried what they will do if I don't turn up cos, they got me to nick stuff,' he said. 'Well, you are just going to be brave and tell them you don't want to a part of their gang.' 'Can't, I'm scared,' Billy said. 'I will come with you to give you Dutch courage.' 'What's that?' 'You will see,' she said. The following day, Billy stood outside the station, nervously looking over his shoulder at me, I was standing by the newsagent. Alan and the boys came along boisterously, right Billy 'boy,' he shouted, jabbing him. Billy looked at him, gathering courage he heard himself say, 'No, I've just come to tell you that I'm not going to be your bag carrier.' Alan was a bit taken aback. Billy said, 'You guys might be thieves, but I am not, you encouraged me to leave my home to have fun, there is no fun in stealing and upsetting people.' Alan said, 'Billy, Billy, mate where is this bravado coming from?' The others laughed. Billy heard himself say

'You are all losers, I don't want to be a loser, that lady from my Unit,' Billy said pointing at me, 'Is going to help me sort myself out.' 'That lady,' Alan said pointing at me laughing, she is a nobody.' 'Don't be so rude,' Billy said walking towards me, 'let's go Miss,' he said. Alan followed making a grab for Billy, he slipped knocking into a tall man. The man turned grabbing him, he looked at him, realising Alan was holding his wallet, 'You are a thieving git,' he shouted, 'Someone call the Police,' Alan writhing to free himself had no idea how the wallet came to be in his hand. He watched as his friends scarpered. Folding my wings, I walked, unseen and led Billy away from the bustle. Out of sight I opened up, 'Gosh Billy.' 'Miss,' he shouted, 'Did you see that?' 'I certainly did Billy and I saw how well you spoke up for yourself.' 'To tell the truth, that's probably the Dutch courage you gave me.'

'What's your name Miss?' he asked. 'It's Angela,' I said as we walked Billy told me that he had made a terrible mistake in leaving his home. 'You just have to behave yourself and be grown up.' I spoke

The following day Billy went to the office and asked to speak to Angela, he was told that they did not have an Angela and he was shown a notice board with photographs of all the staff. As he turned his bed down that night he found a large feather on top of the sheets, the address for the youth club and paper planning his week and explaining how things worked?

George

'George, George, oh my God, why won't you listen?' George looked at his mother and grinned, 'Put that down, it will break if you drop it.' George looked at the colourful plate in his hand, 'Can I, have it?' 'No, it belongs to Jenny.' James who stood watching turned to his brother Howard and said, 'He does not listen anyone.' Howard grinned as if remembering his younger self. Looking at him Howard asked him, 'Hey George, what do you need that plate for anyway?' George turned and looking at Howard asked, 'Why do you want to know?' Howard not having an answer scratched his head giving him time to think said, 'The party is over, what are you going to put on the plate?'

To be more defiant, George held the plate on his head and started running around the room pretending he was an aeroplane. 'Brat,' James said, 'I hope I never have such an obstinate child.' Knowing that he had the attention now of the whole room. George started diving in and out of the tables as adults tried to clear up, they moved swiftly out of his way not wanting to be the one to cause him to crash. James walked over to George's father; his mother had taken herself out of the picture by going into the kitchen to help pack stuff. 'So, what are you going to do then?' James asked. 'I am going to sit here until he gets tired or hungry, one or the other.' He shouted for his wife but there was no response.

I stepped forward from the shadows, 'George!' I said He stopped, stood still and looked at me, as if angry that his fun had been stopped, I could feel his eyes boring into me. 'George, will you please put that plate on the table where it belongs?' Nathan looked at the plate, then the table and walking forward placed it on the table. 'Thank you, George,' I said. 'You really should listen to your mum and dad, what you were doing was dangerous. You know if you had fallen, you would not only have broken the plate but could have injured yourself.' 'Well,' George said, 'The other kids were looking at me and wanted to join the fun.' 'No Nathan,' I said, 'They were looking at your bad behaviour and wondering why you were embarrassing your parents. You made them feel bad.' 'Yea, I guess I should have stopped,' he said, 'I didn't mean to make them feel bad, perhaps if they would take a bit more notice of me, I wouldn't have to play up to get their attention,' he said. I pointed to his dad, 'That new baby that your dad is feeding needs him more than you, do you need feeding?' George looked at me, 'Ok, I guess the baby needs more attention.' As I walked away, I heard George say to James, 'Why does that lady have wings?' As James turned, I stood looking at George and smiled, 'What lady?' James asked, 'That one over there, she told me off.' James looked at George and said, 'That could only have been an angel.'

The Guides

I am standing in a glade, a blue lagoon to my right and a large bench beneath the trees to my left; I am all alone. From the corner of my eye, I saw a tall well- dressed man; we are looking at each other, I have seen him before, but I cannot remember where. 'Hello,' I said, he was silent. 'I've just said hello,' I said, still he was silent, 'Are you not talking to me?' putting hands in his pocket, he leant against a tree. From the left I heard someone say, 'You can't keep going back, you have to move forward,' I turned to see a lady sitting on a bench.

She was dressed in yellow and seemed to glow. 'Stop looking back, you are getting nowhere, you've got to sort your life out.' I stood mouth agape but unable to speak. 'Your garden is full of roses dedicated to people, they're gone, move on.' With thoughts of my parents and friends, I felt a sudden sadness, yes, they had gone.

She of no name was now standing, 'Reach for the stars,' she said. Where is my voice? I was speechless, I looked directly at her; her eyes were like stars, she took my hand, held my gaze and smiled, 'Where is my voice? I'm here to help you be brave.' Suddenly I found my voice, 'Where do I begin?' The man nodded. Suddenly I was awake, opening my hand, I was clutching a star I watched it flow to the sky.

I had been lying on a lounger, under the apple tree in the garden. I had been feeling quite angry, you know like you do, you get the feeling that life , can be mean no matter what you do it does not work. I hated the people at work, especially my boss who took pleasure in not listening to me, the house needed repairs, there was just a small wage to contend with. My son, who had recently left college was finding it hard to get a job. I was beginning to feel really tired as the branches of the apple tree swayed over my head. Looking up, I remember watching a robin pecking a ripe apple, there were several in the garden, but I was wondered if he was a visitor as a drifted off.

I had drifted off to sleep and now lying here, I am trying to understand my dream, who was the man and why was he just standing there, was he telling me I was wasting my time or was it my son who was wasting his time? The lady has said sort my life out. I got up wandered around the garden looking at the roses and then wandered into the house. I sat in the kitchen drinking a cup of tea, I heard the front door slam and then the shout, 'Mum, where are you?' 'In the kitchen,' I replied. Danny stood big grim across his face, 'Cracked it,' he said, 'I went to that big garden centre in Havok as I was wandering around, there was this guy leaning against a tree, I asked him if there were any jobs going. He said, 'walk with me' and he showed me around the garden centre explaining about the trees and plants, then he said 'now go and find the manager.' 'Mum, the manager asked me the garden questions, the guy in the park had given me all the answers; I've got a job as trainee forester.' I went back to thank the guy, but he had gone and no one seemed to know him. I got up and hugged him, 'well done,' I said.

The following week as soon as I got into the office, I noted the huge pile of papers in my in-tray. My boss was sitting on a colleague's desk both chatting and laughing, I turned walking out of the office and made my way to The Human Resources Office. I knocked at the door and was asked to enter. I took a deep breath, I reeled off my details and stated how long I had worked for the Company. The Manager, Mrs Brown, sat and listened, she then retrieved my file from the cabinet. I watched as she read through it. Mrs Brown then turned to me and said, 'Do you mind if I give you a little test?' 'Fine by me,' I said.

Having done the test, I sat, a bit nervous and was called back into the office. 'Well, your qualifications were very out of date; there is a position in the Finance Department for an Assistant Manager, which I feel would suit you, are you interested?' 'Yes please,' I said. 'OK,' Mrs Brown said, giving me a pile of papers, 'You take the rest of the week off and work through these introductory forms etc and report to Mr Shipley, the Finance Manager, on Monday morning. I will sort your transfer.'

I went back to my office, my manager was still sitting on the desk chatting, 'Forgotten where you work?' she shouted at me. I did not respond, I quietly cleared my desk of my personal effects and slid out of that office. I found my voice and my son found a job; dreams do come true.